Don't Make

NOISE

Lose With

POISE

This Book Belongs to:

_____

_____

For Margot, James, and Hank
With Love

ISBN: 9798300918170
Library of Congress Control Number: 2024924347

Don't Make
NOISE
Lose With
POISE

WRITTEN BY David Farkas

ILLUSTRATED BY
Brittany Farkas

If you play a sport, a game,
    or have a running race,
there is one thing that's certain,
    something all of us must face.

Sometimes you'll **win** and that is great,

but sometimes you will **lose.**

And when you lose,

how
will
you
choose
to act

and to behave?

Will you throw a **fit**,

stomp your feet,
and be **unkind?**

Will you let your **anger** win,
    or contain it with your mind?

No one wants to **lose**,
   and it feels lousy to get **beat**,

but controlling our emotions is a **must** when we compete.

The only way
to **never** lose
is to **never** play,

but you'll also

never,

ever,

ever,

win that way.

Losing is a part of playing.
It's a sad possibility.

But that's the way life works sometimes—
that's **reality**.

You don't have to like it,
      but in case you **lose**,
you can't cry and carry on.
      That's not a nice thing to **choose**.

      It takes a lot of strength to lift your head
         and lose with **poise**.
      Doing right is hard to do.
         It's easy to make **noise**.

What is **poise**?

What does it mean,
this word you may have never seen?

Poise just means you're **cool as beans**—

under pressure, you're **serene.**

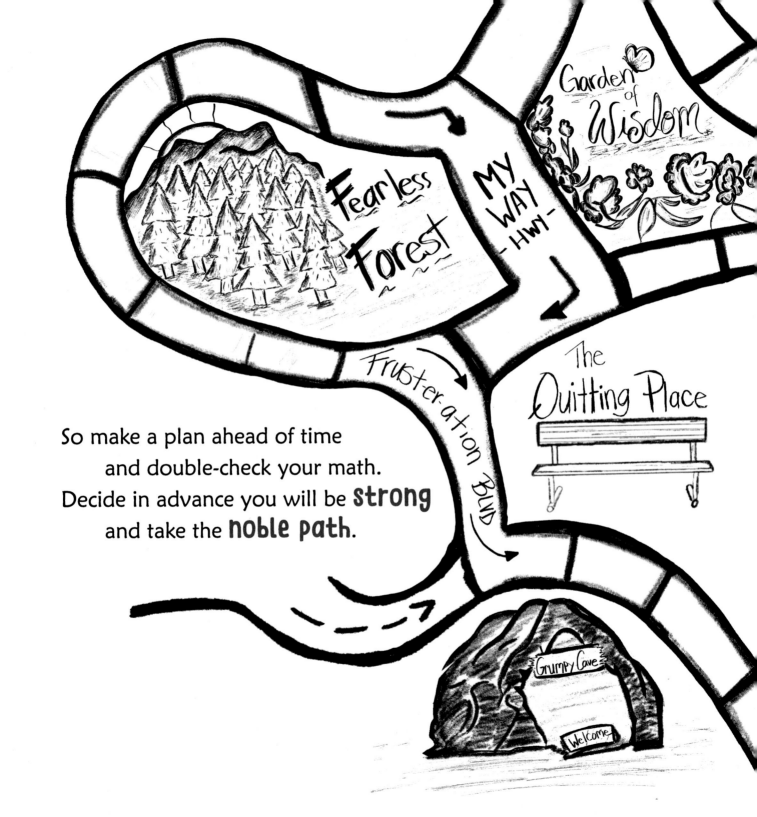

Fearless Forest

MY WAY
—HWY—

Garden of Wisdom

Fruster-ation Blvd

The Quitting Place

So make a plan ahead of time
    and double-check your math.
Decide in advance you will be **strong**
    and take the **noble path.**

Grumpy Cave

Welcome

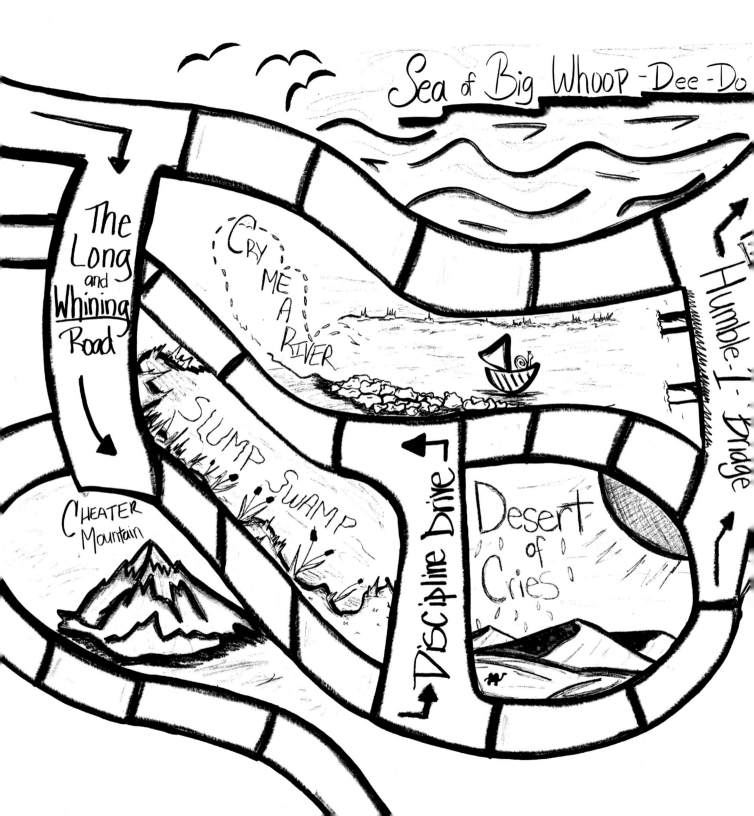

Shake hands with your opponent.

If you're feeling **mad**,
 you won't ruin all the fun.
You don't want to rob the winner
 of his joy of having **won**.

Pay attention, now, to this last,
important move.

The game you lost is done,
now you **learn and improve.**

Learn the lessons from the match
to make you a **better player**,

and use the loss as fuel.
Be a **doer**, not a **sayer**.

Take all the **angst** and **frustration**
that wells up inside

and use it to propel you toward **improving**
all the time.

Be the **best** that you can be.
That's all that you can do.

And if you've done your best, you see,
there's nothing left to prove.

Hard Work · Learn · Grow · Achieve

With your shoulders back and head held high,

each and **every**
time,

don't make noise, lose with poise,

and you will be just fine.

If you lose...

DO

- ☑ Maintain Poise
- ☑ Shake Hands
- ☑ Say "Good Game"
- ☑ Practice Hard to Get Better

If you lose...

DO NOT

- ☒ Cry
- ☒ Scream
- ☒ Give Up
- ☒ Quit the game